The Story of King Arthur and His Knights

Retold from the Howard Pyle original
by Tania Zamorsky

Illustrated by Dan Andreasen

Sterling Publishing Co., Inc.
New York

Library of Congress Cataloging-in-Publication Data

Zamorsky, Tania.
  The story of King Arthur and his knights / retold from the original story by
Howard Pyle ; abridged by Tania Zamorsky ; illustrated by Dan Andreasen ;
afterword by Arthur Pober.
    p. cm.—(Classic starts)
  Summary: An abridged version of the adventures and exploits of King Arthur
and his knights at the court of Camelot and elsewhere in the land of the Britons.
  ISBN 1-4027-2534-5
  1. Arthurian romances—Adaptations. [1. Arthur, King—Legends. 2. Knights
and knighthood—Folklore. 3. Folklore—England.] I. Andreasen, Dan, ill. II.
Pyle, Howard, 1853–1911. The story of King Arthur and his knights. III. Title. IV.
Series.

PZ8.1.Z284St 2006
398.2—dc22

                                                                    2005015519

                          2 4 6 8 10 9 7 5 3 1
                      Published by Sterling Publishing Co., Inc.
                   387 Park Avenue South, New York, NY 10016
                          Copyright © 2006 by Tania Zamorsky
                      Illustrations copyright © 2006 by Dan Andreasen
                        Distributed in Canada by Sterling Publishing
                    $^{c}/_{o}$ Canadian Manda Group, 165 Dufferin Street
                          Toronto, Ontario, Canada M6K 3H6
              Distributed in Great Britain and Europe by Chris Lloyd at Orca Book
              Services, Stanley House, Fleets Lane, Poole BH15 3AJ, England
                 Distributed in Australia by Capricorn Link (Australia) Pty. Ltd.
                          P.O. Box 704, Windsor, NSW 2756, Australia

                            Sterling ISBN 1-4027-2534-5

              For information about custom editions, special sales, premium and
                 corporate purchases, please contact Sterling Special Sales
                 Department at 800-805-5489 or specialsales@sterlingpub.com.

CONTENTS

✎

Prologue

In ancient days there lived a king named Uther-Pendragon who ruled over all of Britain. In beating his enemies, Uther-Pendragon relied strongly on two men in his court. One, Merlin the Wise, was a powerful wizard who was able to see the future. The other, Sir Ulfius, was a noble knight who had led many great wars.

King Uther-Pendragon's wife, the gentle Igraine, had two daughters from another marriage. One of the daughters, Morgana le Fay, was a famous witch. Soon Igraine had a baby boy.

When Merlin came to meet the child, he stood over the baby's cradle and shut his eyes. "Lord," he told Uther-Pendragon, "I am sorry to tell you that I see bad things in the future. You will soon become sick with a fever and die. I see your kingdom falling into great confusion. Your baby's life will be in great danger from enemies that would try to take what is rightfully his. I beg you, let Ulfius and me take the baby away. We will hide him in a safe place until he is grown!"

Uther-Pendragon had great faith both in Merlin's advice and in the gifts he thought his son would someday bring to the world. And so, he let Merlin and Ulfius take the child and hide him. Shortly after that, Uther-Pendragon indeed became sick and died. Just as Merlin had seen, the kingdom fell into a state of confusion. A thousand lesser kings wanted to rule. A thousand other knights and barons hid by the sides of highways. From there they attacked and robbed helpless travelers. Almost eighteen long years passed like this. The land positively groaned with the trouble that lay upon it.

Finally, the Archbishop of Canterbury called Merlin to him. "Merlin," he begged. "Some say you are the smartest man in the world. Surely you can use your gifts to find us a new king so that we may enjoy happiness as we did in the days of Uther-Pendragon?"

Merlin shut his magical eyes again. After a while he spoke. "My lord," he said, "I am happy to tell you that I see great things in the future. This country shall soon have a new king, and he shall be even wiser and greater than was our old friend Uther-Pendragon. He shall bring order and peace where there is now confusion and war. And, best of all, this new king shall be Uther-Pendragon's own flesh and blood."

The Archbishop was very happy, but he was confused. "Merlin," he asked, "when will this new king come? And how will we know him when he arrives? How will we tell him apart from all of the others who would do anything to rule in his place?"

Merlin had a twinkle in his eye. "Do you trust me?" he asked. The Archbishop nodded. "With your permission," Merlin continued, "I will set into motion a grand adventure. By the time it is over, the court will know its rightful king."

Merlin waved his hands and there appeared before him a huge marble stone. When he waved his hands once more, an anvil of solid steel appeared upon the block of marble. Merlin then pushed a large blue sword into the anvil. The sword was bright and shiny. Its gold handle was carefully carved and held many precious stones. And on the blade itself were carved the following words, in letters of gold: WHOEVER SHALL PULL THIS SWORD OUT FROM THE ANVIL SHALL BE THE RIGHTFUL KING OF BRITAIN.

At Merlin's request, the Archbishop announced a contest to everyone in the land. At Christmas, any man who wanted to could try to pull the sword from the anvil. Whoever was able to do so would be the new king of Britain. The kingdom buzzed with excitement. Many people thought King Lot would become King. Some people thought that King Urien of Gore would be King. Others believed King Leodegrance of Camiliard would be the one to free the sword. Still others said that it would be King Ryence of North Wales.

When Christmas came, it seemed like the entire world had found its way to London for the contest. The highways and inns and castles were bursting with travelers. Kings and lords, knights and ladies, esquires, pages, and men-at-arms all came to watch history being made.

Looking out at the crowd, the Archbishop of Canterbury confessed his excitement. "Merlin," he said, "I would be very surprised if we could not find one person worthy of being king among all of these well-known kings and noble lords!"

Merlin only smiled. "My lord," he said, "you may very well be surprised. The one *truly* worthy person may very well still be unknown."

The Archbishop thought about Merlin's words, and so starts this magical story.

CHAPTER 1

How Sir Kay Fought at London Town, Broke His
Sword, and Was Given a New Sword by Arthur

⚬

Among the many worthy men who came to London for the contest was the noble knight Sir Ector of Bonmaison. Sir Ector brought with him his two sons. The elder, Sir Kay, had already shown great bravery and promise. The younger, Arthur, was still a young boy of only eighteen. He was currently serving as Kay's esquire-at-arms. This was very much like a knight's assistant.

Sir Ector and the boys brought with them a great staff. They had beautiful tents of green silk that had been decorated with the family crest.

When they arrived at the field where the contestants were to gather, they were not alone. There were kings and dukes with their courts and no fewer than twenty thousand lords and ladies. There were so many flags and banners that the sky was totally hidden.

Watching the scene, the Archbishop of Canterbury smiled. It was going to be an amazing event. The men would not only be competing on Christmas Day to pull the sword out from the anvil. There would also be a contest at arms to be held during the three days before the sword pull. To this contest the Archbishop invited all knights who were of noble enough birth, condition and quality to compete.

Sir Kay, of course, was found fit and he was entered into the contest. The young Arthur was very proud of his brother. He was happy to carry Kay's flag before him onto the field of battle.

When the day of the tournament arrived, the

audience sat so closely together that the field seemed to be fenced in by a solid wall of human souls. At the Archbishop's signal, a single herald came forth and blew a strong trumpet blast. The doors at the opposite ends of the field were opened and the first two parties of knights entered. They filled the field with their shining armor and other accessories. At the herald's second trumpet blast, the knights leaped toward each other with their spears drawn.

The whole earth seemed to groan beneath the straining feet of the knights' war horses and the roar of the clashing and breaking spears. When the first battle was over and the knights had left, the field was covered with pieces of broken metal. The crowd, realizing it had been holding its breath, seemed to exhale as one. The field was cleared for the next round.

Sir Kay had done very well during that first round. At one point he had held off two opponents at once. Because of this, he was sure that he was ready for the second round. This one was to involve swords instead of spears. The herald blew his trumpet again and the knights were off. Almost instantly Sir Kay proved himself again. This time he held off five opponents at once.

Maybe here, however, Sir Kay grew too confident. When a huge and powerful knight, Balamorgineas, approached and challenged him, the youthful Sir Kay laughed and accepted at once. Swearing to beat Balamorgineas just as he had the others, Sir Kay hit his rival in the head with his sword. He hit Balamorgineas so hard upon his helmet that Balamorgineas's brain swam about in his head. Unfortunately, as Balamorgineas recovered and grew less dizzy, Sir Kay realized that his sword blade had snapped in two. He was left with no weapon.

"Arthur," Sir Kay cried, "quick! Rush to our father's tent and get me another sword!" Arthur

ran as quickly as he could, but when he arrived at the tent he found no one and no weapons there. Suddenly he remembered a certain sword he had seen pushed into an anvil nearby. Surely, he thought, that sword would suit his brother's purposes very well.

The guards were gone when Arthur arrived at the church where Merlin's sword and anvil lay. They, too, were watching the contest. There was no one to stop him as he hopped up onto the block of marble, bent his body, and drew the sword with wonderful ease. Wrapping the sword in his cloak, he ran to bring it to his brother.

When Sir Kay saw the sword, which of course he recognized, he was so stunned that he stood perfectly still. It was as if someone had magically turned him to stone. Finally, he stuttered, "Where did you get that sword?" Arthur, who was completely innocent, explained, and Sir Kay, who was not so innocent, decided. What he decided was that he would say he had pulled the sword from the anvil himself. "Tell no one about this," he told Arthur, who once again innocently agreed.

Sir Kay, however, did want to tell someone. "Go get our father," he said. Arthur ran and asked Sir Ector to come quickly, for he had never seen Sir Kay look quite that way. "Surely something important has happened," he said.

When Sir Ector arrived he saw that Arthur was right. His eldest son's face was as white as ashes of wood and his eyes shone brightly. "Oh sire," Kay said. "I must show you something wonderful." Sir Kay took his father by the hand and brought him to a table, on which he had rewrapped and laid Arthur's sword. Sir Kay pulled back the cloak to show his father the shining metal.

Sir Ector knew the sword at once. "How did you get this?" he asked his son.

Sir Kay stalled. "I broke my original sword and then got this one instead."

"My son," Ector exclaimed, "if you drew this sword out from the anvil, then you are the rightful king of Britain. But if you indeed drew the sword out, you should just as easily be able to push it back in. You will need to draw it out again, with witnesses."

Sir Kay was troubled. "Who could push a sword into a solid block of iron?" he wondered. Why, that would be a miracle! But if his brother, who was nothing special, could pull it out, then surely he, who felt himself to be much more special, could push it in and then pull it back out as well.

CHAPTER 2

*How Arthur Performed the Miracle of the Sword
and Discovered His Birthright*

When back at the anvil, which was still
unguarded, Sir Kay unwrapped the sword from
the cloak. He set its point upon the anvil's iron
and pushed with all of his strength. But to no
avail. After a few minutes, and after he had turned
almost purple from the effort, he gave up.
"Father," he confessed. "No man may perform
this miracle."

"Could I try?" Arthur asked.

"By what right?" said Ector.

"By the right that I drew that sword out in the first place, for my brother," Arthur said. He was not bragging, only stating a fact. He was still innocent, you see, with no understanding of the contest or of its meaning. He did not know why his father looked at him so strangely now. "Are you angry with me?" he asked.

Sir Ector told his younger son that he wasn't angry and asked his older son to hand the sword over. Both father and eldest son watched as Arthur hopped upon the marble block and easily pushed the sword back in. Then he pulled it out and pushed it in again, performing the miracle twice.

Sir Ector gasped and kneeled. He clasped his hands together as though praying.

"Father," Arthur cried, dropping the sword and running over.

"I am not your father," Sir Ector said. And Arthur's face fell. Sir Kay's face had fallen, too, but his at the thought that his brother, instead of him, might actually be king.

Sir Ector cleared his throat and began to tell a story. The story had started eighteen years ago, he explained. The Wizard Merlin and the knight Ulfius had brought him a baby. They had not told him what baby it was, only that he must name that child Arthur and raise him as if he were his own. This he had done.

Sir Ector had never guessed who Arthur's father might be, he said. But today it seemed quite clear. Surely no other baby but Uther-Pendragon's could have performed such a miracle. Arthur was the true king.

"Why are you crying, my child?" he asked Arthur.

"I am crying because I feel as though I have lost you," Arthur replied. "And because I would rather have you as my father than be king."

At that moment, as if by magic, two men appeared. It was the wizard Merlin and the knight Ulfius themselves.

"I have seen all that has happened today in the surface of my magical looking glass," Merlin explained. "I have been waiting for it to happen for eighteen long years."

Taking Arthur's hand in his own, Merlin told Arthur what his future held in store for him. "You will be the greatest and most famous king who ever lived," he said. "You will have many excellent knights gathered around you. The world will talk of your deeds and adventures until the end of time."

"Will you promise me something?" Sir Ector asked the boy, suddenly no longer his son.

"Of course," Arthur replied.

"When you are king of Britain, will you give your brother Kay a position in your kingdom?"

"Of course," Arthur repeated, "but only if you will be my father forever."

Arthur sealed this exchange of promises with a kiss upon his father's forehead and also upon both cheeks. Both men would keep their promises.

And this is how Arthur first discovered he was king. Listen to learn how the world discovered it as well.

ᥣᠣ

By Christmas morning, the day of the contest, thousands of people had arrived to watch the challenge of the sword. A platform had been built around the cube of marble, and a fancy throne had been set out for the Archbishop.

The rules said that, at least in the first round, only those with a natural right to compete should do so. Nineteen kings and sixteen dukes immediately stepped forward, including Kings Pellionore, Lot, Urien, Leodegrance, and Ryence. Each of them tried, some of them several times, but all of them failed. This made them feel angry and embarrassed. The audience was surprised, too. If these great men could not accomplish this task, they wondered, who could?

"You have been tricked by Merlin!" the kings and dukes told the Archbishop. "This task is impossible. Merlin has played a trick to make fun of us all! In your wisdom, you must choose a new king from one of us. Once you have chosen him, we will promise to follow him."

The Archbishop almost agreed, but he could not believe that Merlin would have made such trouble. "We will be patient just a little while longer," he said, "for the time in which it will take a man to count to five hundred, two times.

If no one has pulled the sword out by then, I will do as you ask."

"One, two, three, four, *thank you!*" the kings and dukes cried, counting very quickly.

"Four hundred eighty, four hundred-eighty-one, four hundred eighty-two, *Arthur*," Merlin and Ulfius eventually called. They were enjoying the suspense and had waited until the last minute.

"Who are these men walking with Merlin and Ulfius?" the crowd wondered aloud, as Sir Ector, Sir Kay, and Arthur approached just before the deadline. Merlin brought Arthur to the Archbishop's platform. "Sir," he said, "I have brought you the next contestant for the sword challenge."

"By what right do you bring him?" the Archbishop asked.

"By the right that he is the true son of Uther-Pendragon," Merlin answered.

The crowd gasped. Merlin had taken the boy so quickly that none of them had ever known Uther-Pendragon's baby had been successfully born. Merlin patiently explained, and Sirs Ulfius and Ector faithfully backed up his story. The Archbishop gave Arthur permission to try.

Just as he had done before, Arthur now laid his hands upon the sword, bent his body, and pulled. All the world watched as the piece of metal slid smoothly out of the anvil. As this time was even more exciting than the last, Arthur raised the sword over his head and swung it around three times in joyful celebration, so that it flashed like lightning.

The crowd went wild, shouting so loudly that the whole world seemed to shake. At their cries, Arthur replaced the sword and pulled it out twice more. He performed the miracle three times in total.

The kings and dukes watched in amazement.

Compared to them, Arthur was just a boy. Some of the great men, including King Leodegrance, were happy for Arthur and accepted him immediately. Others, however, including Kings Pellinore, Ryence, Lot and Urien, were bitter. They wanted to challenge the result.

Sirs Ector and Kay stood off to the side. Each one was feeling confusing emotions of his own. Just a few moments before Arthur had indeed only been a boy—a son and a brother. But by performing the miracle again, he had immediately turned into a man.

The crowd strained to touch Arthur, if only to reach a piece of his clothing. But, seeing the emotions on the faces of the only family he had ever known, Arthur pushed through the crowd to reach Sirs Ector and Kay. He took their hands and kissed each one gently on the cheek. The crowd cheered even more loudly then. Arthur's heart and soul were so happy that the pair seemed to take wing and fly like a graceful bird.

Watching this magic, Merlin made a wish—namely that all who might ever hear this story, including you, would realize that they too may succeed in the things they try. They need only passionately pull the sword of their dreams out from the solid iron of their situation. Think about that, won't you, as this story continues.

Conclusion

୧ର

Of course, things are rarely that simple, and this was no exception. Arthur did not immediately become king. While many were happy finally to have peace in the troubled land, others still refused to accept the outcome. Instead they demanded that Arthur go through further trials.

For the sake of peace, the Archbishop agreed. He ordered a second sword challenge at Candlemas, where the entire process was repeated again. There was then a third challenge at Easter and a fourth at Pentecost. After the fourth trial, most people were not only convinced, but by then loved Arthur completely. Finally the Archbishop made it official.

With Merlin's help and good advice, Arthur built a great and powerful kingdom called Camelot. He also made friends of other kings. While Arthur's few enemies remained and waged war against him, he was able to hold off their attacks and win the wars. He drove his enemy King Pellinore away from his possessions and into the forest. King Ryence was driven into the mountains. To prevent attacks from other possible enemies, such as Kings Lot and Urien, Arthur took some hostages of peace. He held Lot's sons, Gawaine and Geharris, and Urien's son Ewaine. They were not prisoners, but members of Arthur's court.

As peace settled upon the land, Arthur's greatness, as greatness will, began to attract more greatness still. Men of noble souls and great skill, who also wished to achieve glory at arms in the courts of chivalry, began to gather around the king. These worthy men would be known as the Worthies, the Knights, or the Ancient and Honorable Companions of the Round Table. Their noble stories shall also follow.

CHAPTER 1

*How an Injured Knight Appeared at
King Arthur's Court, How Griflet Tried to Help,
and How the King Was Sorely Wounded When He
Went to Get Revenge for Them Both*

One warm spring day, Arthur and his court
were making their way through the Forests of the
Usk. Among the knights then present were the
Sirs Gawaine, Ewaine, Kay, and Pellias.

The men stopped to find a patch of shade to
rest in when, suddenly, there came through the
trees a sad sight. It was a bleeding knight being
held on his horse by a golden-haired page.
Arthur's men gathered around to help. They
demanded to know what had happened to their

guest, whose name turned out to be Sir Myles of the White Fountain.

The page told them that he and Sir Myles had gone out one day in search of adventure. They had come upon a valley where three beautiful women were tossing a golden ball to one another. The women had pointed them to a stone bridge crossing a violent stream. There, the women had assured Sir Myles, he would find enough adventure to please any man.

He and Sir Myles had gone to the bridge, the page explained. Far beyond was a dark castle with a tall, straight tower. Just on the other side of the bridge was an apple tree. Its branches were hanging low with a large number of shields. In the middle of the bridge was a single black shield. Beside it was a hammer of brass. Next to the shield was a sign that read: WHOEVER STRIKES THIS SHIELD DOES SO AT HIS OWN RISK.

Sir Myles had grabbed the hammer and hit

the black shield. The castle's great doors had fallen open and a knight dressed entirely in sable armor had come charging out to the center of the bridge. For Sir Myles's boldness, the knight had said he would take away Sir Myles's shield and hang it with the others in the apple tree.

Of course, Sir Myles had fought back. He was seriously wounded and soon lay quietly in the dust. The Sable Knight had reached down, taken Sir Myles's shield, and hung it in the apple tree. He then turned and rode back to his castle. The page had led his master away through the forest until they came upon Arthur.

Arthur thought it was very impolite to leave a fallen knight upon the ground and to take away his shield. All of the other knights agreed.

A boy named Griflet was particularly upset by this story. Jumping up, he begged Arthur to name him a knight. He wished to go back to that bridge and fight the Sable Knight. Arthur hesitated. After all, Griflet was only an untrained boy. But, perhaps remembering his own youth, Arthur eventually agreed.

Griflet left early the next morning. He was gone for the whole day. When he returned, he explained that he had also encountered the three women, had also been sent to the bridge for adventure, and was also left wounded and bleeding. His stolen shield now hung somewhere in that tree.

The Sable Knight had not wanted to fight someone so young and untrained, and had politely lifted the wounded Griflet back up on his horse, but Arthur didn't care. Angrily, he swore that the Sable Knight must be punished. This time, he would finish the task himself.

Early the next morning, Arthur put on his armor. He climbed onto a white horse and set off for that valley where he would find the women playing catch. When they saw Arthur, they stopped playing and walked over to him. When he, too, asked them for their advice for a man seeking adventure, they begged him not to seek it quite so fast. Rather, they invited him to stay and visit with them for a little while.

"Alas, I cannot," Arthur explained. "I must go and find the rude Sable Knight. He has hurt my friends and taken away their shields."

A few miles farther into the dark forest, Arthur came upon a smoky spot. Three sooty men with knives in their hands were threatening an old man with a beard as white as snow.

With an angry sword, Arthur quickly drove the men away. Upon turning to ask the old man if he was all right, Arthur realized the old man was none other than the wizard Merlin.

"Why, it seems to me that I have saved your life!" Arthur exclaimed.

"Do you think so?" the wizard asked. "Take me with you as you continue this adventure.

Perhaps I shall offer you some help as well."

Arthur and Merlin rode for a while. They found the violent river, the bridge of stone, the lonely castle in the distance, and the apple tree hung with both clean and bloody shields. Arthur hit the Sable Knight's black shield so strongly that it was as if twelve shields had been hit at once. When the Sable Knight came out, he and Arthur fought violently. Both men were amazed at the great skill and power of the other.

This went on until Arthur's sword broke. The Sable Knight, seeing this, hit Arthur with one final blow to the head. The powerful blow went through Arthur's helmet, making his brains swim like water and causing him to fall. When the Sable Knight let his guard down, however, Arthur tackled him. Grabbing his helmet and unlacing it, Arthur saw that his enemy was none other than King Pellinore, whom Arthur had driven into the forest. Arthur was so surprised at this that he also let his guard down. Pellinore tackled him in return. He would have finished him off, too, had Merlin not stepped in, saved Arthur's life, and taken the seriously injured king away.

CHAPTER 2

How Merlin Brought King Arthur Away from the Field
of Battle, How the King Found a Noble Sword, and How
He Again Fought with It and Won That Battle

⁓

Merlin brought Arthur to a part of the forest where there lived a holy hermit, known for his ability to heal. Together, Merlin and the hermit gently removed Arthur from his horse. They bathed his wounds in pure water and laid him upon a soft couch of moss to rest.

The next day, the hermit received some more visitors in the form of the Lady Guinevere of Cameliard and her court. They, too, had with them a suffering man. When Guinevere learned of the wounded knight, she asked to be taken to him. She had in her court a very skillful healer, often used to cure the hurts of knights injured in battle.

When Guinevere was brought to Arthur's side, it seemed to her that she had never seen quite so noble a knight. And as Arthur looked up at the lady, it seemed to him that he had never seen quite so beautiful an angel. The Lady Guinevere offered Arthur not only the famous healer, but a box filled with soothing cream to help heal his injured body. Guinevere had to leave right after that, but her visit did the trick. Arthur was much uplifted in heart and, within three days, was entirely healed.

Arthur vowed he would never forget Guinevere. He would not forget his unfinished battle with King Pellinore either. Arthur was sure things would have gone differently if only his sword had not broken. He wanted to try again, but the fight had left him without any weapons.

Merlin told Arthur of a magical place—the Lake of Enchantment. In the very center of the lake, a woman's arm had often been spotted holding the brightest and most beautiful sword in the world. It was many times more amazing than the sword that Arthur had pulled from the anvil. This sword was known as Excalibur. Many a knight had drowned trying to get hold of it.

"I want to try," Arthur said, and the men set off. After a long journey, they found the lake. It was surrounded by lilies and daffodils. Almost at once, a woman's arm came out of the water. She was holding the most beautiful sword Arthur had ever seen. It was made of pure gold and many beautiful jewels.

Just then a fairy approached. Her silky jet-black hair was so long that it brushed the ground as she walked. Arthur got off his horse to greet her and learned that she was Nymue, chief Lady of the Lake. Because she sensed something good in him, she told Arthur a secret. She and the other ladies had created the lake to hide the beautiful castle that lay beneath from human eyes. She also told Arthur that there was only one way a human could ever cross the lake without dying.

"Will you show me?" Arthur asked.

"No man may win that sword," Nymue replied, "except he who is beyond fear and blame."

Arthur sighed, for although he tried to be brave, he often scolded himself. Still, he told Nymue, he wanted to try. That was all she needed to hear. Arthur thought he would need to swim, but Nymue blew a whistle and a magical boat appeared at the shore. That boat took Arthur into the center of the lake. From there, he was able to reach out and take the sword no knight before him had even been able to touch. Just like that, Excalibur was his.

With that great sword, Arthur returned to the bridge made of stone and beat King Pellinore. He was able to do so, in fact, without getting even so much as a single scratch. Toward the end of the fight, King Pellinore begged Arthur for mercy. He promised to surrender if Arthur spared his life.

Arthur decided he would not only spare King Pellinore, but would give back his power. In exchange for this, Arthur asked Pellinore to give two of his sons, Sirs Aglaval and Lamorack, as more hostages of peace. The boys would go on to become famous knights.

On the ride home, the wizard Merlin revealed that Excalibur's sheath was as magical as the sword. The man who wore it would suffer no wounds in battle. Arthur was angry, feeling that this fact took away all the glory of his fight with Pellinore.

However, Merlin gently reminded him that he was not only a great knight but a great king. His life and future belonged to his people. Therefore, he should not take unnecessary risks.

Arthur understood and he swore to protect both the sword and its case. Until, that is, he lost the case through the trickery of someone who should have, by all rights, been his dearest friend. But that is a story still to be told.

CHAPTER 1

*How King Arthur Went to Cameliard and Disguised
Himself for a Certain Purpose and How He
Fought with the Duke of North Umber*

One day, while Arthur was hosting a huge feast
with all of his great court around him, a messenger appeared from the west country. "Lord," he
cried breathlessly, "I come with a message from
King Leodegrance of Cameliard. King Ryence of
North Wales is making terrible demands and
threatening war. He needs your help."

"What demands is Ryence making?" King
Arthur asked.

"He wants land," the messenger explained.
"He also wishes the Lady Guinevere, the king's

daughter, to be given into marriage unto Duke Mordaunt of North Umber."

The entire court shivered upon hearing this, for all knew Duke Mordaunt to be an ugly man with a violent temper.

King Arthur was seized by a great anger. Remembering how Guinevere had come upon him like an angel while he lay wounded in the forest, he swore to help her and her father. The next day, he and Merlin set off for Cameliard, along with the knights, Sirs Gawaine and Ewaine, Pellias and Geraint.

When he and Merlin were alone, the king confessed his feelings about the Lady Guinevere. Arthur asked Merlin to give him a disguise so that he might secretly watch her. He also wished to find out what danger the kingdom was in without being seen. Merlin gave him a cap that, when put on his head, turned the king into a simple country boy. Wearing the cap, that simple country boy was quickly hired to be a gardener at Lady Guinevere's castle.

The Lady Guinevere walked in the garden every day, but the only person she ever saw was the newly hired gardener-boy working in the roses. After working so hard, Arthur needed to wash his face in the garden's fountain. The fountain was in a sheltered spot where Arthur thought he could not be seen.

He was wrong. Watching him from a castle window was Mellicene of the White Hand, one of Guinevere's attendants. She hadn't seen Arthur take off the cap, but she did see a handsome knight, wearing a royal golden collar, bathing. Mellicene ran to the garden to investigate, but Arthur heard her approaching and quickly replaced his cap.

When she asked the gardener-boy about the knight she had seen at the fountain, Arthur respectfully replied that he had been alone there

for the past hour. "You must have been dreaming," he said.

Guinevere said the same thing and Mellicene
was beginning to think it had been a dream. But a
few mornings later she looked out her window
and saw the handsome knight at the fountain
again. She rushed to wake up Guinevere.

Looking out the window with her own
sleepy—but not dreaming—eyes, Guinevere
saw the knight as well. Quickly dressing, she
took Mellicene with her and went down into the
garden.

This time, the ladies came more quietly.
Arthur did not hear them until the last minute.
Although he had time to replace his magical cap,
he realized too late that his golden collar still lay
on the grass. When he said that no one but he had
visited the fountain for an hour, Guinevere knew
it was a lie.

"Take that collar," she told him. "Give it back

to the knight who dropped it and tell him that it isn't polite for knights to hide themselves in a lady's gardens." With that, she and Mellicene went back into the castle. When Guinevere reached her room, however, a thought came to her. She asked Mellicene to go command the gardener-boy to bring her a basket of roses.

When the disguised Arthur entered bearing the roses, all of Guinevere's attendants gasped that he was so rudely still wearing his hat. "I cannot take off my cap," Arthur said, "for...I have an ugly spot on my head."

Guinevere seemed to accept this explanation, but when Arthur bent down to deliver her roses, she reached out and snatched the cap off, revealing him in all of his golden glory. Nobody present knew that they were in the presence of the great King Arthur, but Guinevere did remember Arthur as that wounded knight she had come upon in the forest.

Guinevere was proud and she did not want to swoon over a knight who had lied to her, no matter how handsome he was. She swore that she would protect him and commanded everyone who had witnessed the magic to keep his secret. But for now, she decided, she would put him in his place.

"Take thy cap," she told him coldly, "and go back to your roses, gardener-boy." Her ladies-in-waiting giggled. And with that, she dismissed him. Arthur respectfully replaced his cap, bowed humbly, and left.

❧

The next day, a messenger came to King Leodegrance with news. King Ryence, still demanding land and threatening war, was on his way. Duke Mordaunt, who was still demanding that the Lady Guinevere be his wife, was with him.

Trying to avoid a war, King Leodegrance greeted them as friends when they arrived at the outer reaches of his kingdom. They, however, refused to come inside. Having brought with them a large group of knights and lords, Ryence and Mordaunt instead decided to camp right there, outside the castle walls. They would remain for five days, they told King Leodegrance. If Guinevere did not marry Mordaunt within that time, they would consider Leodegrance to be their enemy and attack.

Although they had allowed five days, Mordaunt decided he was bored after only five minutes had passed. Thinking the Lady Guinevere might be watching and wanting to show off, he challenged any knight in the court to a competition. Puffed up, he rode up and down the field in front of the castle, yelling, "Come on now, is there really no one who will challenge me?"

No one dared to come forth. After all, he was Duke Mordaunt of North Umber, one of the most famous knights of his day. And there was simply no one in King Leodegrance's humble court who could match him. No one, that is, except a simple gardener-boy.

Before he could do anything, however, Arthur had to find some armor. A kind merchant in town supplied him with a noble white warhorse and a fine suit of white Spanish satin and armor. When Arthur, thus fully dressed in white, rode back to the castle, nobody recognized him. But they certainly turned to watch him pass, so obviously noble was he.

His first stop was the Lady Guinevere's castle. Telling her that he was about to do battle in her name, Arthur asked her for a token to carry with him. Guinevere gave him the necklace of pearls that she wore around her throat. Arthur wrapped the necklace around his arm, and he was off.

The Duke Mordaunt didn't recognize Arthur either, for there was no crest upon Arthur's borrowed white armor to give any hints. And upon being thrown from his saddle by the impact of Arthur's skillful spear upon his shield, Mordaunt didn't know what had hit him. Thereafter, he lay very quietly and out of breath for about two hours.

CHAPTER 2

How King Arthur Came Across Four Knights in the Forest and How the Knights Served the Lady Guinevere

⌒

While waiting for Mordaunt to recover, Arthur decided to take a ride into the forest. There he found a knight singing to three ladies in a tower. When he got closer, Arthur realized that the performer was none other than Sir Geraint, one of the knights he had brought with him to Cameliard.

Geraint, however, didn't recognize Arthur and therefore challenged him to a friendly contest of skill. In fact, he bet Arthur that the ladies watching were more beautiful than Arthur's lady. Telling Geraint that his own lady was the most beautiful woman in the world, Arthur accepted the challenge. The men agreed that whoever won would serve the other's lady (or, in Geraint's case, *ladies*) for seven days.

Geraint was a skilled knight but was, of course, no match for the great King Arthur and was quickly overthrown. Arthur helped the surprised knight to his feet. He told him to make his way to Guinevere. He should tell her that he had been overthrown by the knight to whom she had given her pearl necklace. Geraint, who was a man of his word, obeyed.

As Arthur continued to make his way through the forest, he also encountered the three other knights he had brought with him. Gawaine and Ewaine were together, and Sir Pellias was last. Just like Geraint, all three knights challenged the man, whom they did not recognize as their king, to contests of knightly skill. And just like Geraint,

all three knights performed nobly but were overthrown and sent on their way to Guinevere. All
were sent with that same message, that they had
been defeated in her honor by the knight to
whom she had given her pearl necklace.

When the four knights arrived at Cameliard
and realized that each had suffered the same fate
at the hands of the White Knight, they were so
embarrassed that they could hardly look at one
another. However, when Guinevere saw the four
knights whom her mystery knight had defeated,
she beamed with pride and pleasure that she had
given a token of affection to such a great man.

With his magic cap back on and his borrowed
white horse and armor safely hidden in the forest,
Arthur returned to Cameliard. There he found
himself in trouble. His boss, the head gardener,
was angry at Arthur for disappearing when there
was work to be done. Grabbing Arthur by the

collar, he scolded him and threatened to hit him with the stick he was holding.

Arthur's royal spirit surged up within him and he roughly pushed the head gardener away and took the stick away from him. The head gardener went straight to the lady Guinevere to complain.

Guinevere seemed less angry than amused. Secretly, she was thinking it very strange that when the White Champion was around, the gardener-boy was not, and when the gardener-boy returned, the White Champion was missing once more. She wasn't certain, but she thought it too great a coincidence that the gardener-boy and the White Knight had arrived in the kingdom at the same time. She wondered if they might not be the same man. "Let him be," she said, smiling.

She would stop smiling soon. The next day, Duke Mordaunt of North Umber returned.

Having recovered from his first round with the White Champion, he was back with new demands. It was a mere accident, a stroke of bad luck, he said, that he was defeated before. Tomorrow he would come back with six knights for a new challenge. King Leodegrance could also bring seven knights to compete and, if Leodegrance's knights won, Mordaunt would give up his demands. If Leodegrance's knights lost, however, not only Guinevere but all of Leodegrance's kingdom would be his.

King Leodegrance didn't know what to do. Even if he knew where to reach the White Champion, there were no other knights to help him. Surely he, alone, would be no match against Mordaunt and six other men.

Guinevere, who was passing nearby and overheard her father, called her four knights to her and asked them to accept Duke Mordaunt's challenge. To her surprise, Sir Gawaine refused.

"We are pledged into your service," he said rudely, "not your father's. We have no argument with Duke Mordaunt. Finally, we serve King Arthur and can only take on such fights upon his order."

The Lady Guinevere blushed angrily. "Perhaps you are afraid to fight Duke Mordaunt," she suggested.

Now it was Gawaine's turn to blush with anger. "You are lucky you are a woman," he said in a low voice, before turning and walking away.

Guinevere walked away as well. And yet, on her way back to her castle, she bumped into someone. It was the head gardener and he had a message.

"My boy," he explained, in an amazed daze, "has taken his disrespect to an even greater level. Now he has dared to send me to you with a command."

"A command?" Guinevere asked. "To me, from the gardener-boy?"

Taking a pearl necklace out of his pocket, the head gardener nodded. "Yes. Asking me to give this necklace to you, he commands that you prepare him a grand feast and then send the four knights to serve him on silver plates." The head gardener shook his head. "Surely, you will punish him now?"

But Guinevere recognized the pearl necklace as the one she had given the White Champion. "No," she said again. "I shall do as he asks."

Sir Gawaine was angry. "She is punishing us," he told the other knights angrily, "for refusing her earlier request. Very well, we will do as she asks, but once we start serving the gardener-boy, we will no longer be in her service. Our promise to serve her will have been moved, by her own action, to him!"

To the knights' surprise, the gardener-boy seemed quite comfortable around them. Far from seeming frightened, he acted almost as if he thought himself better than them. In fact, once he was finished eating he leaned back and comfortably gave them another command. He told them they were to clothe themselves in complete armor and to ride behind him into battle.

"If you don't watch out," Gawaine warned, "you are going to get it."

The gardener-boy merely smiled. "I don't think so," he said. And with that he pulled off the magical cap, revealing his true identity.

The four knights laughed aloud and kneeled down before their king. After a few minutes, however, they got up. They had a battle to get to!

CHAPTER 3

How King Arthur Beat King Leodegrance's Enemies,
and Revealed His Own Royalty

༚

The next morning, King Leodegrance watched helplessly as the Duke of North Umber arrived with his six promised knights and several heralds and esquires. A crowd gathered to watch the great battle.

But it could hardly be a great battle, Leodegrance thought, when he had no knights to match up against the Duke of North Umber's men. He used to have knights in his court long ago, but since King Arthur had taken control, peace had settled upon the land and the knights had gone where they were needed.

Watching her father, the Lady Guinevere urged him not to give up hope. Somehow, she just had a feeling...

In the next moment, all watched as the mysterious White Knight came riding back into town. Behind him, incredibly, were the four famous knights—the Sirs Gawaine, Ewaine, Geraint and Pellias—that everyone already knew and recognized.

"We are saved," Guinevere whispered. As if hearing her, King Arthur and the four knights all raised their handkerchiefs in a salute as they passed beneath her tower.

"I did this mysterious White Knight the honor of fighting him before without knowing his name or station," the Duke of North Umber said nervously. "However, this is a more serious battle.

If he wants to fight me, he will identify himself!"

"He is not only good enough to fight you," Sir Gawaine promised, "but trust me, it is he who does you the honor."

The Duke of North Umber tried again. "Well," he said, "you are only five, no match for our seven. Yes, that's the reason I will not fight you!"

"Please trust me," Gawaine said, "when I tell you that we five are an equal match for your seven."

The Duke of Umber turned bright red with embarrassment. The fight began. And very quickly, the fight ended. Just as Gawaine had promised, King Arthur's five were more than an equal match for the Duke of North Umber's seven. Mordaunt was defeated and died in what would become one of the most famous battles in the history of King Arthur's court.

The people of Cameliard cheered and celebrated their great victory. They wanted to fuss over the White Knight, but he had disappeared once more, leaving only the four knights for them to congratulate.

The next morning, however, it appeared that they had all celebrated too soon. Far from surrendering, King Ryence was making more demands. Through a herald he had sent a message, King Ryence not only commanded King Leodegrance to surrender his lands, but he also demanded that Leodegrance deliver the White Knight who had killed Duke Mordaunt.

King Leodegrance spoke with great pride. "Tell your king that I will not deliver to him so much as one blade of grass from my land. And I would not deliver the White Knight to him, even if I did know who he was!"

The herald sighed. Obviously King Ryence had anticipated this response, for the next part of the message was that Ryence would soon be coming with a great army to take the things he wanted by force.

King Leodegrance called for Guinevere. "The great White Champion has now saved us twice," he began. "People say this knight is your own particular champion and that he wore your necklace during battle. Is that true?"

Guinevere blushed and nodded.

"Pray tell, then, daughter. Where can we find him? We need his help again! And you are getting to the age where you need a husband, someone to defend our kingdom from its enemies!"

"Father," Guinevere said, "I will lead you to the only man connected to all of this that I know." And with that, she led her father straight to the gardener-boy.

"What is this, daughter?" King Leodegrance asked, as King Arthur's four great knights also gathered around. "Are you mocking me? Is this some kind of joke?"

Guinevere asked the gardener-boy to remove his cap. Arthur did so and King Leodegrance immediately recognized him and called him by name. Guinevere, who hadn't before realized that the golden knight she had seen was King Arthur, kneeled down, horrified. Oh, to think of the ways she had spoken back to him and challenged him!

Arthur, however, made her stand back up. He told her that he loved her and asked if she loved him too. (She did). He kissed her. (She kissed him back.) King Ryence brought the war he had promised, but was no match for King Arthur and his men. Very soon thereafter, Arthur and Guinevere made plans to be married.

As a wedding gift, and at Merlin's suggestion, King Leodegrance gave Arthur a very special piece of furniture. The Round Table, originally made for Arthur's father, was an enormous circular table with fifty seats. When the right knight appeared to take his seat, his name would magically appear, carved in gold on the chair. When that knight died, the golden letters would fade at once.

One of those fifty seats, Merlin told Arthur, was different from the rest. That was a seat known as Seat Perilous. It had this name because if anyone other than the true knight for whom it was meant sat there, he would die a sudden and violent death.

When Uther-Pendragon died, he had left this table to his friend King Leodegrance. A few knights did sit at the table for some time, but lately the knights had all gone. The great table had been put away in the basement, sadly unneeded and unused.

"This table," Merlin promised, "will increase the glory of your reign. Your fame will never be forgotten." And listening to Merlin, Arthur's eyes grew as round with excitement as the table. The table, and great glory, would be his.

Conclusion

༚

King Arthur and The Lady Guinevere were married on a beautiful fall day in a ceremony of great splendor. The kingdom was decorated so beautifully that the whole world seemed to be alive with bright colors. When the Archbishop of Canterbury pronounced them man and wife, bells rang out throughout the land. The king and queen came forth, shining like the sun and the moon.

Also on that day, the Round Table was officially filled. Partly by magic and partly by skill, Merlin had brought the table up from the basement and had built a pavilion to hold the famous piece of furniture. The pavilion's walls were made of gold and painted with the figures of saints and angels. Overhead, Merlin had created a painting that looked like a blue sky covered with stars. Under their feet was a cool floor made of the finest marble stone.

Arthur was about to sit in the Seat Perilous, but Merlin stopped him. "No, sire," he said. "No man but one on the earth may sit in this seat, and that man has not yet been born." Merlin directed Arthur to the seat directly opposite the Seat Perilous, also a beautiful seat, taller and more finely decorated than the rest. "Behold, King," he said, "this is the Seat Royal, considered the table's center seat because you are indeed the center of all that is most worthy of true knightliness."

As Arthur sat, letters of gold appeared as though instantly carved into the chair:

ARTHUR, KING. He was thrilled. Clapping his hands, he invited the many great knights who had gathered as guests at his wedding to take seats at his fine and gracious table.

Merlin, however, stopped him again. "No, sire," he said gently. "Although you have certainly gathered around the noblest court of chivalry in all the world, your table shall not be completely filled today." Merlin assured Arthur, however, that his table would be filled very soon. Walking around, Merlin selected only thirty-two knights who were so far worthy of this honor. Among others, he chose Sirs Pellinore, Gawaine and Ewaine, and Sir Ulfius. Keeping Arthur's promise to his father, Merlin also pointed to Sir Kay. Soon, Merlin had filled the thirty-two seats.

Thereafter, Merlin managed to fill most of the remaining seats. The seat to the right of King

Arthur, however, still remained empty, as did the Seat Perilous.

"Be patient, my king," Merlin advised. "Those chairs' rightful owners shall come in time, and shall be the greatest knights in all the world."

At this, and with the table nearly full, all of the knights stood, raised their swords, and recited in solemn unison what would become the motto of the Round Table: "We, the Knights of the Round Table, will be gentle unto the weak, courageous unto the strong, and terrible unto the wicked. We shall defend the helpless, hold all women as sacred, be merciful to all men, and defend and support each other until the end."

Each man swore to the truth of this vow, and then kissed the blade of his sword to seal his promise. Thus was the great Round Table established.

Prologue

Just what are worthies, you might wonder? Good question. They were three very excellent, honorable lords of King Arthur's court: Merlin the Wise, Sir Pellias, and Sir Gawaine, and in this book we shall tell their stories one by one.

CHAPTER 1

*How Morgana le Fay Planned Evil Against King
Arthur and Sent a Young Girl to Trick the Wizard
Merlin and How Vivien Planned Merlin's Downfall*

Merlin has already been mentioned as a helper
to King Arthur. But he also had a story of his own.
The story of a man so wise, yet so weak, that he
finally tricked himself. Listen to how that happened, and learn.

In a long and dangerous battle with five
enemy kings, Arthur lost eight great knights.
After a period of sadness, Arthur had to choose
other men to fill the eight empty seats of the
Round Table.

He decided he would choose four old and

skilled knights and four new knights, and so he carried on until only one new knight's spot remained. Over this spot, he was torn between two knights—King Pellinore's son, Sir Tor, and his half sister Morgana le Fay's son, Sir Baudemagus. After much careful thought, Arthur decided that Sir Tor's greater deeds in chivalry made him the better choice.

At this announcement, Morgana le Fay leapt up from a nearby seat. "What?" she cried. "You would choose Sir Tor over Sir Baudemagus, my son and your own nephew?!"

Arthur apologized, but stood firm to his decision. He felt that it had been the right choice. Morgana le Fay and Baudemagus remained angry, however, and both left the kingdom. Baudemagus went to seek different adventures and Morgana le Fay went to seek revenge from afar.

Arthur, not knowing her plans, sent his half sister off in style to the isle of Avalon. Morgana le Fay had certain magical powers, which Merlin had taught her when she was a beautiful young girl. One thing he had not taught her was how to see into the future. Nevertheless, she knew for certain that she could never get even with Arthur if Merlin was around.

But Morgana le Fay had a plan. She found a beautiful young girl named Vivien, who was without any heart, being cold and cruel to all who didn't give her her way. Vivien also, Morgana le Fay knew, greatly wanted wisdom.

"I can help you get the knowledge you seek," Morgana promised. She explained that Merlin, with all of his amazing powers, also had a large weakness—his love of beauty. Morgana also revealed Merlin's biggest secret. Although he could see into anyone else's future, he was blind to his own.

"I will trick Merlin with my beauty!" Vivien

swore. "I will make him teach me everything! And once I have all of his wisdom and magical powers, I will cast a spell on him so that he will be made powerless!"

"It is wonderfully evil," said Morgana le Fay, smiling.

Morgana sent Vivien off with a secret weapon: two rings that would unite their wearers' hearts forever. Vivien swept into King Arthur's court during the middle of a party. Having already put on one of the rings, she presented the other one as a challenge. She said that only the wisest and most worthy man there could wear it.

King Arthur tried first, but the ring shrunk so when he touched it that it would not even slip over the tip of his finger. All the other knights tried as well, but with no luck. Finally, Vivien stood before Merlin, the only man in the room who had not yet tried the ring.

Merlin was suspicious, but he could see no future that involved himself, and Vivien was very beautiful. Merlin tried on the ring and found that it fit, and he was pleased and proud. When he tried to slip off the ring, however, it stuck to his finger as if part of his skin.

Immediately, he knew he had been tricked. But almost as quickly, the ring started working its magic and he forgot all about everything except Vivien's youth and beauty.

"How can I prove my love for you?" he asked her.

"You can give me your wisdom and teach me your magic," Vivien replied.

And the lovesick old wizard did just that.

It took a very long time, but Vivien was patient. Eventually, she learned just about everything Merlin knew, including how to build castles out of nothing more than earth, wind, fire, and sky, and then how to make them

disappear again with just the wave of a wand.

One day she brought Merlin a delicious meal. Merlin could not see that the meal contained a powerful sleeping potion. He ate and began to get very sleepy.

Merlin realized again that he had been tricked. This time, not even his love for Vivien could distract him. Before he fell asleep, he asked Vivien to go and save King Arthur from some coming danger that Merlin could see was about to occur. Feeling strangely guilty and thinking it would lessen her sin, Vivien promised, and Merlin started to snore.

Once Merlin was completely asleep and helpless, Vivien finished him off. She wove a silver web around him so that, even after he woke up, he was unable to move a single muscle. Vivien smiled as her attendants pulled at Merlin's whiskers and beard. Finally, to make sure that he stayed where he was, she placed Merlin into a large heavy box and partially buried it, covering it up with a magical mist.

And this was the shameful end of a very wise, but very weak, old man.

CHAPTER 2

*How Morgana le Fay Returned to
Camelot with a Plan to Harm King Arthur and
What Happened to Sir Accalon*

⚬

Meanwhile, Morgana le Fay, pretending to be humble and sorry, returned to King Arthur's court to beg for brotherly forgiveness. While there, she and Arthur fell into a friendly talk about Excalibur.

"I'd like to take a closer look at it than I have before," Morgana said. "May I?"

King Arthur walked over to Excalibur, which was resting in a place of honor in the corner. He gathered up the sword and the case and allowed Morgana to examine them. He reminded her, as I am reminding you, that the magical blade could cut like no other, and that the sheath protected from wounds whomever was wearing it.

"Oh, brother," Morgana sighed. "Excalibur is so beautiful. I cannot bear to give it back just yet. Do you think I could take it home with me and keep it, just for a little while, so that I may look at it some more?"

Arthur hesitated, but he was so grateful they were friends again that he agreed. Little did he know that the dishonest Morgana would not just take Excalibur home to look at it. Rather, she would hire goldsmiths and armor smiths and jewelers to make an exact copy of it. No one except her would be able to tell the difference just by looking at it.

Soon afterward, Morgana went back to the court to visit. After greeting her warmly, Arthur asked about Excalibur.

"You know," Morgana said, "I forgot to bring

it because I was so excited about the other present I have for you. She told him about the beautiful new black horse she had waiting for him downstairs. As Arthur had been planning to go on a hunt, this worked out perfectly. Asking her to bring Excalibur next time, Arthur thanked his sister and set off.

The horse was so fast as it chased the hounds and hare that it raced well ahead of everyone else's horse but one, that belonging to Arthur's friend Sir Accalon of Gaul. The two men soon found themselves quite alone and lost in a deep and thickly tangled part of the forest. They decided to trust their horses' instincts to take them home, or at least to some other safe place. Arthur's horse took the lead and the men traveled through the night.

The next morning, the horses pushed through the forest and stopped on a beach before a smooth sea. On the horizon, a ship with colorfully stitched silk sails was moving quickly toward them.

On deck, there stood twelve very beautiful women waving. "Come aboard," they cried. "Surely you are hungry and thirsty and tired!"

"What do we have to lose?" King Arthur said. "Perhaps it shall be another great adventure." Sir Accalon agreed and the two men went aboard.

Suddenly the ship began to move out to sea. The men were worried, but they soon became distracted and had an enjoyable evening. At the end of the night, they allowed the women to lead them to sleeping quarters where they would spend the night.

༄

When Arthur opened his eyes, he thought he must still be dreaming, for he found himself in a dark and gloomy dungeon made of stone.

Around him he saw many other knights, moaning and in a sorry state.

One of the knights explained that they were being held prisoner by a knight named Sir Domas. When Sir Domas's father had died, he left everything in his large estate to Sir Domas and his brother, Sir Ontzlake. Over the years, however, Sir Domas had taken almost everything from his younger brother except for one small castle.

"He wants that last castle," the knight said, "but he cannot get it himself and he cannot find a knight to take up his greedy case for him. That is why we are all here, as prisoners. All of us refused to help him."

"I will help him," Arthur vowed, "if only to get free. But then I will *hurt* him, for what he has done."

A woman came into the room then. Arthur recognized her as one of the women who had lured him and Sir Accalon onto the ship. "Did

I hear you say you would defend Sir Domas's cause?" she asked.

"I will take on his cause on one condition," Arthur said. "You must promise to go to Camelot and ask Morgana le Fay to send me my sword, which she is holding."

Morgana le Fay laughed when she heard the message, for of course she had set up the whole thing. She laughed even harder when she gave the woman not the real Excalibur, but the copy she had made.

Now, when Sir Accalon opened his eyes, he was not in a dungeon. Rather, he was in a mysterious pavilion being watched by an ugly dwarf. The dwarf told Accalon that the pavilion belonged to the Lady Gomyne of the Fair Hair, who invited Sir Accalon to breakfast.

Of course, the Lady Gomyne was working for Morgana le Fay as well. While they ate, the Lady Gomyne told Sir Accalon a sad story about a worthy knight named Sir Ontzlake who had an evil older brother.

"Sir Domas has not only taken everything, but has now found himself a Knight to steal Sir Ontzlake's final possession. His one remaining castle," the Lady Gomyne cried, "and Sir Ontzlake cannot defend himself, for he was recently wounded in battle. Please, sir, won't you help?"

"I would," Sir Accalon said, "and gladly. But I have no armor."

The Lady Gomyne smiled and said she would be right back. She returned holding something wrapped in a scarlet cloth. When he unwrapped it, Sir Accalon gasped.

"My lady," he cried, holding what he had no way of knowing was the real Excalibur. "This sword is identical to the sword of my friend and king, Arthur! I will do anything to have it!"

And so it was agreed that Arthur and Sir Accalon would fight each other—Sir Accalon with the real Excalibur and King Arthur with the fake. As each man was wearing the armor and colors of the man for whom they were fighting, they could not see each other's faces. Therefore, they did not realize they were fighting each other.

Vivien arrived just as the battle began. Although her mission was to save King Arthur, she could not tell immediately which knight he was. Very soon, however, it became clear that he must be the knight in greater trouble. And in great trouble he was. Arthur's fake sword barely made a dent in his opponent, while his opponent's sword cut into him deeply. And the case of Arthur's sword, which in the past had protected him from all wounds, seemed to sleep as the blood flowed freely from his body.

Sir Accalon was just about to finish King Arthur off when Vivien stepped in, casting a spell that knocked Excalibur out of his hands. Arthur ran to pick up the other weapon, recognizing it at once as the one that was truly his. When he picked up the case, which had also fallen, all of his wounds stopped bleeding. Almost immediately, Sir Accalon started to bleed instead. Before fainting from blood loss, Sir Accalon removed his helmet and Arthur saw the face of his friend.

Arthur tried to help, but had already lost a great deal of blood and was very weak. As promised, Vivien used her magic to heal Arthur. But she refused to help Sir Accalon, who later died. Saddened, and still not quite understanding what had happened, Arthur gave all of Sir Domas's wealth (except for one small castle) to Sir Ontzlake and then returned home.

Some time later, Morgana le Fay came nervously to visit, worried she had been found out. But when she arrived, Arthur was sleeping. Sneaking into his room, she decided she would try to take Excalibur again. As Arthur was sleeping with the sword under his pillow, however, the only thing she could steal was the case.

When Arthur awoke, found the case missing, and learned that his sister had been there, he finally realized that she had been at the bottom of all his recent troubles.

Vivien offered to help Arthur catch Morgana le Fay, and Arthur accepted. But before they could catch her, Morgana took the case and threw it out into the middle of a vast lake. As she did so, a white arm covered with many gold bracelets rose up out of the lake. The arm caught the case and drew it deep under the water, from which it would never rise again.

Sensing Vivien and Arthur behind her, Morgana disguised herself and her court, turning them all into a bunch of rocks and stones lying upon the ground. Arriving there, Vivien sensed the magic immediately and offered to turn everyone back if only Arthur would promise to kill Morgana as a punishment.

But Arthur refused and scolded her in front of witnesses. After all, Morgana was still his sister. Vivien smiled, called Arthur a fool, and told him gladly what had happened to his good friend Merlin. She then left that place. From that day forward, because he had refused her in public, Vivien hated Arthur even more than Morgana le Fay did.

And thus ends the story of Merlin's presence in Arthur's life.

CHAPTER 1

How Sir Pellias Took Up a Quest on Queen Guinevere's Behalf, Overcame a Red Knight, and Did Battle with Sir Engamore

And now I shall tell you the story of Sir Pellias, who was nicknamed by many, "The Gentle Knight." The story begins with Queen Guinevere, who one day went for a walk with her ladies in waiting and some knights. It was a beautiful day, and they were enjoying their stroll, when suddenly a woman approached them on a white horse. She was joined by three pages, one of whom held a large square object covered in red satin.

The woman's name was Parcenet and she had come from the court of the Lady Ettard for a very specific purpose. The Lady Ettard was considered by many in her court and surrounding neighborhood to be the most beautiful lady in the world. She had heard that Guinevere was also extremely beautiful and had sent Parcenet to find out if this was true.

"And it is indeed true," Parcenet said.

"Why, that is very sweet," Guinevere said, "but funny, to come all this way for so small a matter. Tell me, what is that square object hidden by red satin?"

At Parcenet's nod, the page pulled back the satin to show a portrait of the Lady Ettard.

"If that is the Lady Ettard," Guinevere said graciously, "then she is indeed beautiful as well, much more so than am I."

"Not so, lady!" Sir Pellias protested. "You are the more beautiful of the two, and I would be willing to back up those words in battle."

"You are lucky that we are here and not back

in the Lady Ettard's court," Parcenet said, "otherwise Sir Engamore of Malverat, who is the Lady Ettard's defender, would *force* you to back up those words in battle!"

Sir Pellias decided that he would welcome such a friendly challenge and he begged the queen for leave to do so. Although she still thought the subject matter to be silly, she was flattered and she agreed to the adventure.

Sir Pellias was so eager to get going that he did not even take the time to pack or put on his own armor. He had faith, he said, that he should find armor fit for this purpose somewhere along the way.

While passing through the Forest of Adventure, Pellias and Parcenet's group came upon an old woman sitting on the mossy bank of a deep and violent stream. The woman's eyes were very red, as though she had been crying for years. Her face was thin and wrinkled. Bristles and whiskers sprouted from her cheeks and chin.

Parcenet shuddered. Unlike Guinevere and the Lady Ettard, this old woman was definitely not beautiful, she thought! And so, when the old woman asked Sir Pellias for a ride on his horse across the deep and violent stream, Parcenet told the woman that Sir Pellias was too important to take on such a task.

Sir Pellias, however, gently scolded Parcenet. He reminded her that a true knight helped anyone in need. With that, he got off his horse, lifted the old woman up onto it, and rode her across to the other side.

Once on the other side, the old woman hopped off the horse and was suddenly completely changed. Instead of red eyes, wrinkles, and whiskers, she had black eyes like jewels, ivory skin, and long, silky black hair. Around her neck she wore a beautiful necklace, a collar of opal stones and emeralds set into gold. She was, they all knew immediately, Nymue, the chief Lady of the Lake. Her old woman disguise had merely been a test of Sir Pellias's knightliness.

"You passed," she said, "and for that you have won a prize." Reaching up, she removed the golden collar from around her neck and gave it to Sir Pellias to hang on his shoulders like a medal.

What Sir Pellias did not know was that that necklace was magical. Whoever wore it would be beloved by everyone who looked upon him. The group continued on its way.

∽

The next day, while in the forest, Sir Pellias and Parcenet came across yet another crying woman, this one quite young, and followed by an also sad esquire.

"What is wrong?" Sir Pellias asked.

"It does not matter," she sighed, "for you cannot help me."

"How do you know?" Sir Pellias asked. He gently helped her off her horse, gave her some water, and asked her once more to tell him of her troubles.

The story she eventually told was a sad one. She had been hunting with her new husband, Sir Brandemere, and their beloved dog had run ahead of them across a long and narrow bridge that went over a violent stream. As they started to cross, a terrible knight and horse had come from a dark stone castle on the other side of the bridge. Both the knight and the horse were dressed entirely in red.

Although they had explained to the Red Knight that they only wanted to get their dog back, the Red Knight told Sir Brandemere that he must first overthrow him if he wanted to pass. Sir Brandemere was unarmed and clothed only in light hunting clothes, but he was brave. He had drawn his sword and continued forward. The Red Knight had struck Sir Brandemere on the head, causing him to slump forward over his horse, bleeding heavily. Without a word to the lady, the Red Knight had taken the bridle of Sir Brandemere's horse and led both man and horse over the bridge and into the dark castle.

"I know not whether he is dead or alive!" the woman said, crying again.

"Good lady," Sir Pellias said, "I can indeed help you."

"But you have no armor," the woman said.

"Just take me there," Sir Pellias replied. And the lady did.

As Sir Pellias began to cross the bridge, the Red Knight came rushing across again, demanding to know who dared approach. Sir Pellias explained that he was only there to ask what had happened to Sir Brandemere.

"The same thing that will happen to you!" the Red Knight replied.

"But I am not armed," Sir Pellias said.

"Then I suggest you turn back," the Red Knight replied.

Instead of leaving, Pellias picked up the hugest stone he could find—a stone that five normal men probably could not have lifted. He threw that stone at the Red Knight and knocked him off his horse. He then drew the Red Knight's sword and held it to his neck, demanding information.

He learned that the Red Knight's real name was Sir Adresack and that Sir Brandemere was alive but being held prisoner. Sir Adresack was actually holding about twenty-one other prisoners, having over the years held anyone who had attempted to cross his bridge, taking them captive and demanding great ransoms. Two of these people were actually from King Arthur's court, Sir Brandiles and Sir Mador de la Porte.

Sir Pellias could have killed the wicked and ill-mannered Sir Adresack but, when he begged for mercy, Pellias decided to spare his life. In return, however, Sir Adresack had to give the still-unarmed Sir Pellias his armor, free all the prisoners, and then go to Camelot to beg for forgiveness.

While freeing the prisoners, Sir Pellias found all the riches that Sir Adresack had stolen over the years. Taking nothing for himself, he split everything among the victims. They loved him even more for his kindness than they had already come to love him due to the magical powers of his necklace. They begged him not to leave, but he was on a mission, and, with Sir Brandiles and Sir Mador, he left to continue it.

When Pellias and Parcenet reached the

borders of Grantmesnle, the land of the Lady Ettard, Pellias and his men set up tents. Pellias asked Parcenet to take a message to the lady.

"Tell her, please, that a knight is here to announce Queen Guinevere's greater beauty and to defend that statement against any knight that would challenge him."

Parcenet could not, due to her position, wish Pellias to be the winner in any such battle, but certainly did wish him good luck.

The next day, Sir Pellias put on the red armor Sir Adresack had given him and arrived at the castle prepared for friendly battle. A crowd had gathered. In front of them, the castle drawbridge dropped and someone came out. He was a large and proud knight, dressed entirely in green, and known as the Knight of the Green Sleeves. His real name was Sir Engamore of Malverat and he greeted Sir Pellias politely. He did, however, feel just as strongly about the Lady Ettard as Sir Pellias did about Queen Guinevere.

The men rushed toward each other with great speed and force. Sir Pellias's sword knocked Sir Engamore off his horse and violently onto the ground. Everyone gasped, especially the Lady Ettard, for none of them had ever seen Engamore defeated. Sir Engamore was also unused to losing and was embarrassed and ashamed. Sir Pellias took off his helmet and went to introduce himself to the Lady Ettard.

Once he was standing in front of her, however, he realized that she was several times more beautiful than her picture had been. Due to her great beauty, he fell a little bit in love with her. And, due to the magical collar he wore, so did she with him. Until now, she had always kept Sir Engamore at her side. But over the next few days, she asked for Sir Pellias instead. Sir Brandiles and

Sir Mador de la Porte eventually returned to the tents, but Sir Pellias stayed behind as an honored guest. All the while, Sir Engamore watched sadly and jealously.

"My Lady," Pellias said to the Lady Ettard one night, "what can I do to show you how much I care?"

"You can give me that beautiful collar that you wear around your neck," she replied.

Sir Pellias did not want to part with the necklace, which had been a special gift from the Lady of the Lake, but it pleased the Lady Ettard so much that he agreed to let her wear it for a little while.

As soon as Sir Pellias took the necklace off, the magic stopped and the Lady Ettard began feeling something other than love. She felt angry that she should have been so easily charmed by Pellias and that she had been made to overlook her long-time loyal champion, Engamore. She didn't let on to Pellias that her love for him had faded, but instead continued to laugh and look at him lovingly, all the while planning her revenge upon him.

The Lady Ettard told Parcenet to bring her a sleeping potion to give to Sir Pellias. Parcenet begged her not to, but she insisted. Eventually Sir Pellias ate the poison, which the Lady Ettard slipped into his dinner.

When he was asleep, the Lady Ettard had Sir Pellias stripped of all his clothes except his underwear and taken to a public place outside of the castle. When the sun came up, everyone would gather around and mock him and make him feel the same shame he had made Sir Engamore feel in defeating him.

And that was exactly what happened when Sir Pellias woke up the next day. He sat there, confused, near-naked, and humiliated, until Parcenet ran up with a blanket for him to wrap himself in.

Sirs Brandiles and Mador de la Porte were

very angry at what the Lady Ettard had done and they begged Pellias to let them get backup from Camelot to come and teach the Lady Ettard a lesson.

Sir Pellias, however, refused. For one thing, he told them, the Lady Ettard was a woman. As such, he would defend her honor to the death. For another thing, he confessed, he loved her. Upon saying this, Sir Pellias called out for his esquire to bring him his armor.

"I am going to try to win a visit with her," Pellias vowed. "I don't know what kind of spell I am under, but if I cannot see her and talk to her again, I will surely die!"

Fully dressed in his armor, Sir Pellias rode back to the edge of Grantmesnle and waited. Sent by the Lady Ettard to punish him, ten knights soon approached. Already a great knight and now strengthened by love, Pellias quickly defeated eight of them. The other two were about to turn and run but, just then, Pellias put up his hands and surrendered. They dragged him back to the castle and Sir Pellias smiled secretly, for this was exactly what he wanted. In just a few moments, he thought, he would see his love again. But the Lady Ettard saw him first.

"Do not bring him up to me!" she cried from an upstairs tower as the knights approached with their prisoner. "Put him on his horse, with his hands tied behind his back and his feet tied beneath the horse's belly. Then send him back outside so that everyone can laugh at him again."

When Sirs Brandiles and Mador de la Porte saw this latest humiliation, they begged Sir Pellias even more strongly to allow them to regain his honor.

"I don't care about my honor," Sir Pellias insisted, for such was the power of the magical collar that the Lady Ettard now wore all the time.

"Well, what about the honor of King Arthur and his Round Table?" Pellias's two friends tried instead.

With a great and terrible voice, Sir Pellias replied, "I do not care about them either."

CHAPTER 2

*How Guinevere Quarreled with Sir Gawaine,
and How He Met Sir Pellias and Promised to
Help Him with the Lady Ettard*

ᕤ

While Pellias was off on this adventure over
Queen Guinevere's beauty, another knight was
at Camelot getting on the queen's nerves. It was
Sir Gawaine, whom she had long disliked. She
had felt this way ever since that day, perhaps,
when he had not only refused to help defend her
father's kingdom, but had responded so rudely to
her request. Many people found him charming,
but she found him proud and arrogant. Her heart
had hardened against him.

One day, one of the Lady Guinevere's favorite

dogs jumped on Sir Gawaine with its muddy paws. Not knowing she was watching, Sir Gawaine hit the ears of the dog. Running up, she demanded to know why he had hit her dog.

"Your dog did something to me," Sir Gawaine replied, "and when someone does something to me, I fight back."

Guinevere drew herself up proudly. "Do you forget to whom you are speaking?" she asked. "How dare you?"

Gawaine drew himself up just as proudly. "Perhaps you, my Lady, do not remember that I am the son of a powerful king. And I dare do whatever I must to defend my rights."

All onlookers gasped and looked immediately away. Guinevere stood for a moment, furious, before she spoke again. "Sir Gawaine," she finally said. "You are proud and arrogant beyond measure. I am the queen and this is my court. I command you to be gone and show your face no more until you are ready to apologize to me for the rude way you have always treated me!"

With that, Guinevere turned and walked back to her chamber. Once she was there, however, she wept in secret anger and shame. She hated what had just happened, but at the same time she was so proud that she would do the same thing all over again.

Upon hearing that his cousin was to leave Camelot, Sir Ewaine asked King Arthur's permission to leave the court as well. King Arthur happily agreed, and the two knights set off together in search of another great adventure.

Monks at an abbey told them about a spot in a meadow where a shield hung upon a sycamore tree. The shield, the monks said, was being treated very badly by some ladies. Gawaine and Ewaine thought this very strange, but set off to find the ladies.

Sure enough, they found the meadow, the

sycamore tree, and the shield. Three beautiful young ladies were throwing insults, rocks, and mud at the shield. Its owner, a knight wearing all black, sat silently on his horse saying and doing nothing.

Sir Gawaine charged at the ladies, shouting at them to "Get away!" Flinging one last fistful of mud, they quickly fled. The Ebony Knight approached and, to Gawaine's surprise, asked him why he had interfered. "Why, because they were being disrespectful to what looked to me to be a noble and knightly shield!" Gawaine exclaimed.

"It is my shield," the Ebony beforeKnight said wearily, "and I am perfectly able to defend it. "

"Apparently not!" Gawaine said, challenging the knight. The two men then fought, while all of the people in the castle gathered and looked down over the walls. Gawaine, who had never before been unhorsed by anyone except King Arthur, felt quite confident that he would win the contest.

But before he knew
it, his spear was bro-
ken into many pieces and he was flung out of his
saddle, landing heavily upon the dusty earth.

With his pride injured, Gawaine rushed at the
Ebony Knight with great fury. The Ebony Knight
responded in kind until Sir Ewaine pushed his
horse between the two men and broke them up.

"For shame, Gawaine!" he cried. "To seek
such a fight with a knight who met you in a
friendly fashion in a fair contest!"

Gawaine shrugged and put up his sword. The
Ebony Knight did the same. With peace thus
restored, the Ebony Knight invited Sirs Gawaine
and Ewaine back to his home for some refreshments. It turned out to be a rich and royal home
and the Ebony Knight to be Sir Marhaus, the son
of the king of Ireland. Gawaine was greatly com-
forted that at least he was defeated at the hands
of someone of very great importance.

Marhaus finally explained why he had stood by and not defended his shield. Some time ago having accidentally knocked a knight's lady off a horse and into the water, he had agreed as a punishment not only to stand by and do nothing while the lady's attendants threw insults and earth, but to defend those ladies against the first seven knights who came to defend the shield's honor. Sir Gawaine was the seventh knight and thus freed Sir Marhaus from his duty. Marhaus was now free to join Sirs Gawaine and Ewaine in their search for adventure.

The next day, the men rode through the Forest of Adventure. The silence was so deep that even the hooves of their horses on the ground could scarcely be heard. Following a small deer, they came upon a fountain. Next to the fountain sat a beautiful woman with an ivory face, jet-black hair, and eyes as bright and brilliant as jewels. She was none other than the fairy and chief Lady of the Lake, Nymue.

Nymue told the men that Sir Marhaus would someday be one of the most famous knights of the Round Table. Today's adventure, however, would be Sir Gawaine's. Nymue brought the men to the top of a hill, from which they looked down into a valley and saw a strange sight indeed. It was a knight, dressed entirely in red armor, who alone faced the ten knights who approached him. Impressively, he beat the first eight and the final two seemed ready to turn and run. But just then, the Red Knight did the strangest thing of all. He put away his sword and surrendered to them, and they brought him back to the nearby castle.

"Just wait," Nymue said, and only a few

moments later that same knight was sent back out of the castle with his hands tied behind his back and his legs tied under his horse.

"Now you may go," Nymue told Gawaine. "There is your adventure."

Sirs Gawaine, Ewaine, and Marhaus rode down into the valley where, to their surprise, they saw the tents and the symbols of Sirs Brandiles and Mador de la Porte. The five friendly knights sat and shared refreshments together. But when Gawaine asked them about the sight they had witnessed in the valley, Sirs Brandiles and Mador de la Porte seemed unwilling to answer. Instead they asked Sir Gawaine to follow them to see the answer for himself.

"Sir, you are a knight of King Arthur's royal court," Gawaine said sternly, upon seeing that the red knight was Pellias. "How could you submit yourself, and that court, to such shameful insult?"

Pellias did not reply.

"Sir," Gawaine said fiercely. "Answer me one way or the other, by words or by doing battle with me, for I will not allow such shame to come upon our king without defending him. You and I were once friends, but unless you explain yourself at once, I will consider you my enemy."

When Pellias finally explained, Sir Gawaine agreed that it was as if Pellias had been put under a spell, just as someone had recently done to Merlin the Wise. Sir Gawaine vowed not only to get to the bottom of things, but to regain his friend's honor. He had a plan.

Putting on Sir Pellias's red armor and mounting Pellias's horse, Sir Gawaine rode boldly toward the Lady Ettard's castle. Now, it just so happened that she was at that time walking along an outside wall and saw the red knight approaching.

"Why do you return?" she called down. "Can't you understand that the more you come to me, the more I hate you?"

Sir Gawaine removed his helmet and showed his face. "I am not the man you hate. I overthrew him and took his armor and his horse. He will trouble you no more."

The Lady Ettard was impressed. Sir Pellias was one of the greatest knights in the world, so if this new knight had overthrown Pellias, he must really be a champion. He was also, she noticed, very handsome, with a rich dark beard and hair and eyes as blue as steel. She invited him inside her castle.

All was going well with Sir Gawaine's plan— until, that is, the spell of the magical necklace began to work on him as well. Just as had his friend Pellias, Gawaine began to fall in love. And, because the Lady Ettard now had a great champion, poor Sir Engamore fell quickly into second place again.

After spending many pleasant days there, falling deeper and deeper under the necklace's spell, Sir Gawaine found himself wondering why he should ever leave. After all, he had been forced, unfairly he felt, from King Arthur's court. Why should he not stay with the beautiful Lady Ettard and create a court of his own?

When Gawaine did not return, Sir Pellias suspected that something might be wrong. He disguised himself as a friar dressed in a black robe and made his way to the castle, announcing that he had an important message for Sir Gawaine.

Coming upon Gawaine and the Lady Ettard, and seeing them gazing lovingly at each other, Sir Pellias pulled off his hood, walked straight up to the Lady Ettard, and ripped the magical necklace off her neck.

"It is mine," he cried. "You have no right to it!"

"And as for you," he told Sir Gawaine, "you have betrayed both me and the knighthood!" He slapped Gawaine so strongly that the mark of his ring remained on Gawaine's face.

"Sir," Gawaine said, "I have betrayed you, but the injury you have just given me makes us equal."

"We are not equal," Pellias fumed. "For I injured only your cheek, but you have injured my heart! I will answer to you for slapping you. But you will answer to me for your betrayal!"

"I stand ready to answer to you!" Gawaine promised. Glancing at the Lady Ettard in disgust, for she no longer wore the necklace, he turned to go.

"Yes, go!" she mocked him. "But go with the mark of a greater knight on your face."

"Look at Sir Pellias's face tomorrow," Sir Gawaine vowed, angrily, "and see what mark I will have by then left there."

CHAPTER 3

*How the Lady of the Lake Took Back
Her Necklace from Sir Pellias*

∽

The next day, true to his word in response to the Lady Ettard's taunts, Sir Gawaine challenged Sir Pellias to a fight and Pellias accepted.

Everyone watched as the two great knights and former friends faced each other. The Lady Ettard watched from a distance but, as Sir Pellias once again wore the magical necklace, she found herself wishing that he would win.

The two men crashed together in the middle of the field. At first it seemed that Pellias had won. Sir Gawaine's spear broke and he was pushed forcefully off his horse, hitting the ground as though dead. But as Pellias rode off, he realized that he, too, had been injured. The tip of Gawaine's spear must have pierced his armor and broken off in his side, for he was in great pain and bleeding heavily.

Parcenet and a dwarf happened to be riding through the forest at just that time and came upon the suffering Pellias. The dwarf knew of a holy hermit healer who might be able to help and they carefully brought Pellias to the hermit's home. They arrived too late, however, for Pellias was already in his final death swoon.

"I am afraid nothing can be done," the hermit said.

Just then, the door opened and a beautiful lady strode in. Dressed all in green, with arms covered with bracelets of emeralds and opals, she had an ivory face and her eyes were as sparkly and as black as her hair. The hermit knew immediately that she was no ordinary human.

"Give me just a few minutes with this man," she begged. "I can help him. I promise not to use any bad magic."

The hermit agreed. Once left alone with Pellias, Nymue first took her necklace from around his neck and put it back on her own. Next she pressed a magical stone to Pellias's wound and watched as the spearhead was pulled out. Upon the blood that quickly followed, Nymue pressed a square of magical cloth. Finally, she brought forth a small tube filled with a blue potion. Pouring a drop onto Pellias's dry lips, she watched as the wounded knight came back suddenly from the edge of death. There was no denying, however, that he had come back as someone different.

"Am I dead?" Pellias asked her.

"No," Nymue replied, "but you are no longer what you were. In order to save your life, I had to give you a potion that made you only half-man. You are now also half-fairy."

Nymue now wore the magical necklace and as Sir Pellias gazed upon her he felt nothing but gratitude and love. In fact, as half-fairy, he felt better than he ever had. His body was as light as air and his soul was filled with joy.

"Can I now come to live with you?" he asked. "Since you have saved my life, can I now give you that life forever?"

Nymue whispered, "Since the first time I saw you, that is all I have ever wanted."

The two sealed their new love with a kiss.

Meanwhile, Parcenet and the dwarf, unaware of Pellias's recovery, had made their way back to Grantmesnle with news of his coming death. Sir Gawaine, still weak from his fall, was beside himself with guilt. "First I betrayed him," he said, "and now I will be responsible for his death. I must go and seek his forgiveness!"

Gawaine stopped first at the hermit's home and then continued on in the direction the hermit told him Pellias and Nymue had gone. He was happy to learn that Nymue had healed his friend, but he still needed to find him and make things right.

Gawaine rode until the forest began to grow quite dark. Suddenly, there appeared a pale blue light, seemingly for Gawaine to follow. In that light, which shone brighter and clearer than the moon, Gawaine was able to see every petal of every tall flower that surrounded him. Arriving finally at a beautiful blue lake, Gawaine realized that he must be in the land of the fairy.

Suddenly, he saw Nymue and something that looked like a spirit come out of the lake. Realizing that the spirit was Pellias, Gawaine happily rushed forward to hug him, but Sir Pellias stopped him gently.

Pellias explained to Sir Gawaine that he was now only half-human. He told Gawaine that he loved and forgave him, but that his life would now be something else, something lived with Nymue.

"But where will you go?" Sir Gawaine asked.

"I will be there," Sir Pellias said, pointing to the lake, where Sir Gawaine saw only water, but where Pellias promised there was a wonderful city of gold and blue and fields full of flowers.

Sir Gawaine looked into the face of Sir Pellias and saw that it was now ivory as well, with jet-black eyes that sparkled like jewels. But he also saw true happiness there. Promising Pellias that he would apologize to Guinevere, Sir Gawaine turned to go.

He watched, both sadly and happily, as Pellias and Nymue turned and walked off into the water. Thereafter, Gawaine and the other men returned to Camelot where, true to his promise, he made a fragile peace with Queen Guinevere. Sir Marhaus was made a Companion of the Round Table and went on to become one of its most famous knights. And, with all of the other knights gone and the Lady Ettard looking favorably upon him again, the long-suffering Sir Engamore quickly married her and became the Lord of Grantmesnle.

CHAPTER 1

*How a White Deer Appeared Before King Arthur,
How Sir Gawaine and His Brother Gaheris Went
After It, and What Happened to Them on That Quest*

This final part shall tell the story of Sir Gawaine, who, as you have seen, was sometimes rough and harsh in his manner, but in whom a gentle nature and great loyalty also lay.

One day while King Arthur and his court were picnicking on the grounds, a delicate white deer burst through some distant trees, followed quickly by a handsome white dog. After a bit of a chase out in the open, the terrified deer ran back into the forest, the dog nipping closely at his heels.

Before the court even had a chance to turn back to their food, two other creatures burst noisily from the woods. They were a knight and a lady, dressed as if for a hunt. Finally, a third creature appeared. He was a single knight on a black horse and he seemed angry. Charging at the other knight and striking him with his sword, he grabbed the lady, threw her yelling across his saddle, and rode back into the forest. After a moment, two esquires came, picked up the wounded knight, and led the horses away.

As all of this had taken place quite quickly and some distance away from the picnic site, no one in the court was able to step in. However, King Arthur asked Sir Gawaine to investigate and to take his brother, Gaheris, as his esquire.

The first thing Gawaine and Gaheris found were two knights fighting. It turned out that the knights were brothers, fighting over that very same deer and dog. They had started fighting because one brother was hoping the deer would escape the dog and the other that the dog would catch and kill the deer. Then they'd started to argue over who would be the one to rescue the lady and they were still at it.

Gawaine and Gaheris left those knights and continued on their adventure. The next thing the brothers found was a large castle. The dog lay dead at their feet, hit several times by arrows. Gawaine loved dogs and blamed the deer. When the deer ran by again a moment later, Gawaine caught and killed it. Having seen this from their windows, the lord and lady of the castle came rushing out.

"Oh, what have you done to my beloved deer?" cried the lady, falling weeping upon the ground.

Gawaine apologized, but when the lord hit him with his sword, he found himself surprised and angry. Although the lord begged for mercy, Gawaine raised his own sword to slay him.

What happened next, however, Gawaine didn't intend. As he swung, the lady moved in front to defend her husband. Gawaine tried to turn his swing but his sword still grazed the lady's neck, causing her to bleed and fall down as if as dead as the deer.

Thankfully, she did not die. The lord was so grateful that he forgave all and invited Gawaine and Gaheris to dinner. Over the meal, the lord told them the story of his brother, who had taken his wife's sister as his own wife.

A strange woman, he said, dressed all in red and with red hair, had given one sister the deer and the other the dog. The sisters had been very happy, but, almost immediately, the chase began and the couples clashed. The lord confessed that he had been the angry knight in black who had hit his brother and kidnapped his brother's wife. He had done it, he said, out of revenge and for the honor of his own wife and her deer.

Gawaine was suspicious. The woman the lord described sounded like the witch Vivien, famous for making mischief such as this for pure fun. "Since both deer and dog are now dead," he said, "let your fight with your brother also die."

The lord agreed. When Gawaine returned to Camelot, however, and described to Arthur and Guinevere all that had happened, Queen Guinevere decided *he* was the troublemaker. She privately told an attendant how Gawaine had shown the lord no mercy and how he had struck and injured a woman. "Surely, his sword has now been dishonored," she said.

Gawaine, overhearing this, decided that Guinevere would hate him forever and would never really give him a chance. He hid his anger, however, and—out of respect for the queen—broke his now dishonored sword across his knee.

Don't worry about Sir Gawaine, though. He went on to prove himself, both to Queen Guinevere and, perhaps, to you as well.

CHAPTER 2

*How King Arthur Became Lost in the Forest
and Overcame the Knight-Enchanter, and How Sir
Gawaine Finally Became a Noble Knight*

Some time after this, King Arthur himself craved some adventure. As Queen Guinevere and her court were away in Carleon, it was a good time to go. Taking only a favorite esquire, Boisenard, with him, he set off.

After getting lost for a while in a very dark wood, the two came upon a great but grim castle. A light was on inside and when they knocked a porter appeared.

"We are a worthy but weary knight and

esquire," Arthur said. "May we take shelter here tonight?"

"If you know what is good for you," the porter replied, "you will sleep in the woods. No good comes to knights who seek shelter here."

This made King Arthur curious and he insisted upon coming inside. The porter led Arthur and Boisenard into a room where a lively party was taking place. An old knight sat at the head of the table. He had a white beard and a broad chest. Around his neck he wore a chain of gold with a locket attached. He invited the men to eat.

For dessert, the old knight invited the men to play a game. In a contest of courage, he explained, each competitor would try to cut off the other's head.

"That seems like a strange sport," Arthur said, and everyone in the room burst out laughing, as though in on some shared secret.

"Are you afraid?" the old knight asked.

Arthur angrily replied that he was afraid of nothing and, against Boisenard's pleas, he agreed to play. As he was the guest, the old knight insisted that Arthur must swing the sword first.

Still angry but satisfied to be going first, Arthur drew Excalibur, swung, and, with remarkable ease, lopped off the old knight's head.

"Well, that's that," he said, thinking that he had won.

But to his surprise, instead of falling, the body of the old knight walked calmly over to where his head had landed, picked it up, and placed it right back on top where it was as good as new.

"My turn to swing," the old knight said, and everyone watching laughed again.

The old knight swung once and then twice, but each time stopped just short of hitting Arthur's head. He moved his sword slowly a few more times, pressing the tip just slightly into the skin of Arthur's neck before stopping.

"Cut off my head if you are going to," Arthur said, "but torture me no longer."

"I will do something else entirely!" the old knight cried. "I will spare your life for a year and a day, if you promise to come back at that time for your beheading."

Arthur promised.

"And I will spare your life again at that time," the old knight added, "if you can give me the answer to the following riddle: What is it that a woman desires most in the world?"

Arthur sighed. Now the old knight was really torturing him, for who knew what women really wanted? Was it wealth? Beauty? Pretty things? The power to please? Nevertheless, making Boisenard promise that Guinevere was not to be told, he agreed to the challenge.

A year passed in which, despite asking almost every woman he had come across during that time, Arthur felt himself no closer to knowing what women wanted. Still, as promised, he set out grimly to return to the old knight's castle and his possible death.

Just before he reached the castle, however, Arthur came across an old woman living in a hut built into a mossy oak tree. The poor thing was horribly wrinkled and ugly, with filmy eyes and ears that flapped and only one tooth left in her mouth. Still, Arthur greeted her politely and made one final attempt at getting the answer to his riddle.

"I know the answer," the old woman said, "but I will only tell it to you on one condition. If I guess right, you must promise me that I may choose any knight in your court to become my husband."

Arthur hesitated, not sure that he could make that promise for another man. However, realizing that the only other choice was his death and that his noble knights would do anything to prevent that, he agreed.

"That which a woman most desires is to have her will," the old woman said. She also told him that the old knight was an evil magician who had played this game with many men and who was able to win every time because of the magical gold locket around his neck. When his head fell off, his life went safely into that locket. That was the secret behind the trick.

When Arthur got to the old knight's castle, the first thing he did was recite the old woman's answer to the riddle, word for word. The old knight blinked and Arthur knew the answer was right.

The next thing Arthur did was to reach out and take hold of the magical gold chain and locket.

"Now, old knight," Arthur said, "perhaps we can play another game in which you give me this chain and locket around your neck." Arthur pulled hard. The chain broke and the locket opened revealing a shining ball of crystal that held the old knight's life. Arthur flung the crystal ball roughly onto the ground, where it broke. At this, the evil old magician broke as well, finally falling down dead.

Arthur was eager to get home. Stopping at the old tree hut, he gently gathered up the old woman and set her carefully on the horse in front of him. At all times during the trip, he treated her with the greatest respect, as though she were a beautiful young queen instead of an old woman.

When he arrived home, everyone watched in silent confusion as Arthur told of how the old woman had saved his life and about the promise he had made her in return.

"Was I right to make that promise?" he asked

the knights who stood before him. All of the loyal knights who were present told him that he was. Upon hearing this, the old woman looked the knights over for a while before lifting a bony finger and selecting Sir Gawaine to be her husband. As all watched sadly, Gawaine walked up to the old woman, took her hand, and pressed it to his lips.

The old woman was taken and dressed up in clothes fit for a queen, which in the minds of all who saw her so, made her look even uglier. The old woman and Sir Gawaine were then married in the church of King Arthur's court.

While he was doing his best to do his duty, the proud Gawaine secretly suffered. After the ceremony, Gawaine went into his room and stayed there, wanting to be left alone. By nightfall, however, he realized that he was behaving badly and being rude to his new wife. He went to find her and to apologize.

"I accept your apology," she said. "Now, it is so

dark in this room. Why don't you go get a light?"

Gawaine returned carrying a candle. But when he approached her and the circle of light fell on her face, he saw before him not the old woman he had married but a lady of great beauty with long black hair, eyes like black jewels, and lips like coral.

"Who are you?" Gawaine gasped.

"I am your wife," she replied. "I was only old and ugly because a spell had been cast upon me. But your kindness in marrying me has set me halfway free."

"Halfway?" Gawaine asked.

"I must still remain old and ugly for half the day, but I shall let you choose what half."

Gawaine replied that he did not care what others thought during the day and that he would prefer that she was her real beautiful self at night, when alone with him. But his wife replied that she would rather be beautiful during the day, so as not to have people laughing at her.

"Well then, so be it," Gawaine replied. "You are my wife and I respect you. You shall have your will in this and all other things."

His wife laughed, admitting that she had only been giving him one last test that he had passed wonderfully. She explained that she had been one of the Ladies of the Lake but that she had loved him since watching him bid good-bye to Sir Pellias and that, for his sake, she had become human.

Gawaine invited everyone in the court to come and to bring lights and refreshments. When they arrived, they were overjoyed to learn what had happened and to meet Gawaine's true new wife.

So let this be a lesson to you. Just as Gawaine's

wife at first appeared to him to be something awful, so often does one's duty. But once one has committed himself to his duty, as a groom does with patience to his bride, then so often does that duty become beautiful. I do pray that you may find yourself as worthy of your duty and as happy as Sir Gawaine.

Another time, I shall tell you the story of some other excellent knights. But for now I bid you good-bye.

What Do *You* Think?
Questions for Discussion

᭪

Have you ever been around a toddler who keeps asking the question "Why?" Does your teacher call on you in class with questions from your homework? Do your parents ask you questions about your day at the dinner table? We are always surrounded by questions that need a specific response. But is it possible to have a question with no right answer?

The following questions are about the book you just read. But this is not a quiz! They are designed to help you look at the people, places, and events in the story from different angles. These questions do not have specific answers. Instead, they might make you think of the story in a completely new way.

Think carefully about each question and enjoy discovering more about this classic story.

1. Do you believe King Arthur was a real person? What parts of his story do you think are fact and which are legend?

2. Why do you think Sir Kay acts as he does when Arthur pulls the sword from the anvil? Have you ever been jealous of a friend or sibling?

3. Why does Arthur wish to keep his identity a secret from Guinevere? Have you ever hidden something about yourself? How did you finally reveal the truth?

4. Arthur quickly learns that he must select the knights of the Round Table carefully. If you

were creating your own Round Table, who would you select?

5. Why does Merlin try on Vivien's ring, in spite of his suspicions? Have you ever done something despite your better judgment? How did it turn out?

6. Why does Arthur allow Morgana Le Fay to take Excalibur? Have you ever been tricked by someone you trusted?

7. Why do you suppose the knights are always in search of adventures? Have you ever actively sought out an adventure? Did you find one?

8. Why do you suppose Nymue gives Pellias the necklace? Is it simply a reward, or does she have another motive? Have you ever received a present that wasn't quite what it seemed?

9. Did you guess the answer to the old knight's riddle? Have you ever been asked a riddle that you couldn't solve on your own? What was it?

10. There are three parts to the code of the Round Table—be gentle to the weak, courageous to the strong, and terrible to the wicked evil-doers. Do you agree with the code? Do you know anyone who lives by such a code today?

Afterword

∽

First impressions are important.

Whether we are meeting new people, going to new places, or picking up a book unknown to us, first impressions count for a lot. They can lead to warm, lasting memories or can make us shy away from any future encounters.

Can you recall your own first impressions and earliest memories of reading the classics?

Do you remember wading through pages and pages of text to prepare for an exam? Or were you the child who hid under the blanket to read with a flashlight, joining forces with Robin Hood to save Maid Marian? Do you remember only how long it took you to read a lengthy novel such as *Little Women*? Or did you become best friends with the March sisters?

Even for a gifted young reader, getting through long chapters with dense language can easily become overwhelming and can obscure the richness of the story and its characters. Reading an abridged, newly crafted version of a classic novel can be the gentle introduction a child needs to explore the characters and story line without the frustrations of difficult vocabulary and complex themes.

Reading an abridged version of a classic novel gives the young reader a sense of independence and the satisfaction of finishing a "grown-up" book. And when a child is engaged with and inspired by a classic story, the tone is set for further exploration of the story's themes, characters, history, and details. As a child's reading skills advance, the desire to tackle the original, unabridged version of the story will naturally emerge.

If made accessible to young readers, these stories can become invaluable tools for understanding themselves in the context of their families and social environments. This is why the *Classic Starts* series includes questions that stimulate discussion regarding the impact and social relevance of the characters and stories today. These questions can foster lively conversations between children and their parents or teachers. When we look at the issues, values, and standards of past times in terms of how we live now, we can appreciate literature's classic tales in a very personal and engaging way.

Share your love of reading the classics with a young child, and introduce an imaginary world real enough to last a lifetime.

Dr. Arthur Pober, Ed.D.

Dr. Arthur Pober has spent more than twenty years in the fields of early-childhood and gifted education. He is the former principal of one of the world's oldest laboratory schools for gifted youngsters, Hunter College Elementary School, and former Director of Magnet Schools for the Gifted and Talented for more than 25,000 youngsters in New York City.

Dr. Pober is a recognized authority in the areas of media and child protection and is currently the U.S. representative to the European Institute for the Media and the European Advertising Standards Alliance.

Explore these wonderful stories in our
Classic Starts library.

20,000 Leagues Under the Sea
The Adventures of Huckleberry Finn
The Adventures of Robin Hood
The Adventures of Sherlock Holmes
The Adventures of Tom Sawyer
Anne of Green Gables
Black Beauty
Call of the Wild
Frankenstein
Gulliver's Travels
A Little Princess
Little Women
Oliver Twist
The Red Badge of Courage
Robinson Crusoe
The Secret Garden
The Story of King Arthur and His Knights
The Strange Case of Dr. Jekyll and Mr. Hyde
Treasure Island
White Fang